THE CENTRAL THIEF

DECODING OF THE DEVIL

JEROME SHELTON ALEXIS

ISBN
Paperback 979-8-89744-629-2
Hardcase 979-8-89777-863-8

Dedicated to the relentless Corporate Warriors who are fighting against modern day slavery.

Preface

Why?

That question has haunted me for as long as I can remember.

Why am I sprinting through the deserted streets in the dead of night, with four police officers on my heels? Why is there a bounty of one million rupees on my head? Why did I waste years studying engineering, only to end up in a BPO? (Not that anyone really wonders about that everyone knows the answer.) Why do parents obsess over what the neighbours think? Why did I fall in love with Jennifer?

Why? Why? Why is it always me?

With every pounding step, a fresh "why" claws at my mind. But right now, none of them matter except the one that asks how I'm going to get out of this alive. I can already picture it: my body crumpled in a dingy 10x10 interrogation room, fists raining down, forcing me to confess to a crime I never committed.

I used to scoff at movies that claimed to be "Based on True Events." Corruption, power games, police brutality I had dismissed them as exaggerations. But now, as I run for my life, every scene I once mocked plays out in real-time before my eyes.

This isn't a movie. This isn't a bad dream my mother will shake me awake from with a bucket of hot water. This is real. I've been running for four days now. And the only thing keeping me going is the desperate hope that my family, my friends and Jennifer aren't suffering the same fate.

Life is unfair

Seventy-five percent of people in India believe that. It's unfair when a man earning thousands is asked to pay school fees in lakhs. Unfair when talent means nothing without connections. Unfair when dreams are crushed beneath the weight of loans, corruption, and survival.

I belong to that community the ones for whom life is an endless uphill battle. And yet, I've read stories, met people who claim it's possible to break free.

But can I?

I studied in a government school. Took five years to complete my degree in Computer Science. No campus placement. No desire to work in engineering. I wanted to be a police officer. Instead, life laughed in my face and handed me nothing but disappointments.

My name is Aaron Wyatt. An ordinary man with dreams, dreams I was never allowed to chase.

Of course, there's another side to life a **Fair Community.** The ones who thrive while the rest of us struggle. Strange, isn't it? Same country. Same laws. And yet, while some soar, others sink deeper into the abyss.

"Excuse me, dear partner," my lungs gasp, burning as I push forward. "You're always with me, yet you never listen. My heart is suffocating, pounding like a war drum, and here you are, lost in thoughts about fairness. Can we focus on survival for a second?"

My ankle twists, sending pain searing up my leg. I stumble but force myself to keep moving.

I was never one to take risks. Never invested in stocks. Never burned the midnight oil for an exam I knew I wouldn't pass. Never took loans. Never spoke the truth about what really happened six months ago at the company.

But now?

Now, I have no choice.

The bridge looms ahead. Below, the dark water churns, waiting. The sound of handcuffs clinking behind me is growing louder.

There's no other way.

It's time to let all hell break loose.

Chapter 1

Six Months Ago...

My body begged for sleep, my mind felt like a dull, overworked machine, and my eyelids drooped as if carrying the weight of a hundred sleepless nights. But sleep? It was a luxury I couldn't afford.

The temple next door had rented out speakers loud enough to wake the dead, and the cotton stuffing inside my pillow did little to muffle the relentless chanting tearing through my eardrums. As if that wasn't enough, my parents had chosen this very moment to wage war over breakfast.

"Coconut chutney or tomato?"

At this point, I wasn't sure which was worse, the temple speakers or my mother's furious debate with my father over what should accompany the idlis.

I had always brushed off the so-called social media influencers who preached about the horrors of working night shifts. But now, I was starting to feel it: the constant irritation, the dullness in my senses, the never-ending fatigue, the lack of a proper diet. Worst of all, no one around me seemed to acknowledge it. They still expected me to run errands, pick up groceries, fetch milk packets, as if my exhaustion was invisible.

A sudden, unmistakable urge jolted me upright. Dragging myself to the bathroom, I entered *Incognito Mode*.

(Yeah, don't judge. We all do it.)

There's a strange moment after it's done. That heavy silence. That fleeting regret. Studies say most people feel the same thing, *"I should stop doing this"* or *"Not again"*, as they stare at themselves in the mirror. I wasn't any different.

I wiped my face and sighed.

My name is Aaron Wyatt. Like most engineering students, I had studied engineering without the slightest interest. Ever since I was ten, my dream had been to become a police inspector.

"Why?" people would ask.

I could have given them noble answers, *"To serve the people, to fight corruption, to bring criminals to justice."* But the truth was simpler. I was obsessed with crime thrillers. The way detectives pieced together clues fascinated me. I wanted to be that guy, the one who cracked the case.

But I didn't become a cop. Because I failed the "Cash Test."

(Yeah, if you know, you know.)

So there I was two years out of college, unemployed, with relatives whispering about me at every family gathering.

"What's he going to do?" It's the question every Indian family asks, whether you're struggling or thriving. There's no escaping it. My parents pressured me into attending tech company interviews, and the only thing I got from them was a series of rejections. In the end, I had no choice but to settle for a BPO job.

Oh, wait. *Medical Billing Company.* Gotta make it sound fancy. The salary? A glorious ₹15,000 per month. I was ready to throw away the offer letter. Then, I saw her. Jennifer.

She was in the parking lot, struggling to manoeuvre her Scooty. I walked over to help. She glanced at my offer letter, noticed the joining date, and smiled.

"See you in training."

That was it. That was all it took. I took the job.

A deafening crash snapped me back to reality.

I shot up, my heart hammering. The house was eerily silent. No voices. No movement. Just the shattered remains of our TV screen.

"Am I hallucinating? Is this sleep deprivation or am I dreaming?"

Before I could process it, two familiar arms wrapped around me from behind.

"Happy Birthday!"

Mom. Dad.

"Really?"

I blinked at them, trying to comprehend. My parents, the strict, no-nonsense boomers born in the '60s, were now part of the *Instagram surprise birthday trend?*

"We wanted to do something special for you." My father, Benjamin Wyatt, was smiling, but his voice still carried the weight of a retired Army officer. Strict, firm, disciplined - he had been the embodiment of authority all my life. Even now, despite his attempts to adjust to modern parenting, there were moments when *Colonel Benjamin Wyatt* resurfaced like a ghost.

"My hero, Happy Birthday!" Mom beamed. *"Now that you have a job, my wish is to see you married by your next birthday!"*

Hope Jennifer hears your wish, Mom.

Every Indian household has that one mother: the doting, overprotective, partner-in-crime. The one who saves you from your dad's wrath, sneaks you money for trips, and cries when you're hurt. That was Rebecca Wyatt, my mother.

"Alright, get ready. We're going to church, then lunch." The Colonel issued his orders.

"Dad, I'm exhausted. Can we move this to Sunday?"

"No. We're going today. If you're that tired, take the day off from work."

My brain exploded.

"WHAT?! NO WAY!"

I *had* to go to the office. If not for work, at least for a handshake from Jennifer.

"Fine. But I need to be back by 2 PM. I need at least two hours of sleep."

As I pulled on a fresh shirt, I felt a familiar discomfort.

L to XL. Another year older. Another size bigger. Yeah, birthdays were great. But they were also a reminder that life was moving forward… whether I was ready or not.

Chapter 2

10:30 AM – Santhome Cathedral

They say *"God is everywhere."* And yet, every Sunday, millions of people make their way to temples, churches, and mosques. I never really questioned it before, but at this moment, standing inside Santhome Cathedral on a sleep-deprived brain it felt like a legitimate contradiction. *"If He's everywhere, why do we need to come here?"* Maybe it was the exhaustion talking.

"Aaron! Happy Birthday, my dear boy!"

I turned around, curious to see who was so excited about me getting older.

"Father Patrick! Thank you so much. Bless me, Father."

"God will always bless you. May all your dreams come true and may all your problems leave you this year."

Really? For the third year in a row, I had received the *exact same* blessing. And if I was being completely honest, absolutely nothing had changed.

"Thank you, Father. Shall I?"

"Of course! Go ahead with your prayers. And don't forget to pray for a good bride - that's your mother's wish."

He winked and walked away. I shot a glance at my mom. She gave me a knowing smile. Sighing, I walked through the church, looking for a place to rest. I don't know how it is for others, but my brain operates just fine in normal surroundings. However, the moment I step into a holy place, it starts generating the *most* unholy thoughts. *"Wow, she looks great.", "Maybe I should sit closer to her?"*. I mean, I can manage to pray for about two to four minutes. After that, my mind takes a scenic tour of everything and everyone around me.

And today? Today, my brain decided to tackle an even bigger mystery. *"Why do mothers insist on announcing that their son or daughter needs to get married? Is it some kind of indirect matchmaking strategy? A way of nudging people into recommending someone? Or is it just a warning like, 'If you're not going to help, at least don't interfere'?"*

A light tap on my shoulder pulled me out of my deep philosophical prayers.

"Let's go," Mom said.

"Are you okay?" I narrowed my eyes at her.

"I usually spend an hour in church, but today is your birthday. Let's go celebrate!"

Okay, now I was officially concerned.

"I'm not surprised. I'm scared. Do we need to see a psychologist?"

"Stop joking. Let's leave."

Something was definitely up. First, a surprise in the morning. Now, my parents were cutting *church time* to celebrate? I folded my arms. *Suspicious levels: Rising.*

"Mom, just one question, have you found a bride for me? Are we going to meet her today? Is that why you're rushing?"

She laughed.

"No chance in hell. You at least need a six-digit salary to get married. You know how today's girls are."

Boom. Direct hit.

"Emotional damage! Let's just go. No further questions."

Outside, my dad sat in our legendary 2008 Maruti Suzuki Alto, revving the engine like a race car driver. Except, he wasn't revving it for style. He was trying to keep it from shutting down. I sighed. Many sons feel this way, I think. *"Dad, the road is empty. Can we...maybe... move a little faster?"*

At long last, we reached R & G Park Hotel. It had valet parking, but Dad wasn't letting go of the car that easily.

"Be careful with the car. If there's even a tiny scratch, I'll file a complaint!"

The valet who had probably dealt with *worse* car owners gave a tired nod and drove our Alto into a parking spot. Wedged neatly between a Mercedes-Benz AMG GLC43 and an Audi A4.

Dad told us to head upstairs. As soon as we reached the top floor, the lights dimmed, and BAM!

A shower of glittering paper rained down as loud voices screamed:

"HAPPY BIRTHDAY, AARON!"

For a moment, I just stood there, dumbfounded. Then, I spotted the culprits. Gilbert, my best friend since school, college, and now in Care All Technology. First graduate in his family, landed this job with me because no other company wanted a guy with *questionable English skills*. Hamshad, who *just* joined the company but doesn't care about work because he's flying to UAE in nine months. Mandeep, aka *Gundu*. He only cares about food. Seby, the *mystery girl*. No one knows much about her family. But she gets along with everyone. Yes, we had all joined Care All Technology at the same time. And from Day 1, we were a pack.

Hugs. Wishes. Laughter. But while my ears processed their words, my eyes were scanning the room. Where was Jennifer? I tried not to look too disappointed. Instead, I focused on what really mattered, food. Half Tandoori. Butter Chicken. Butter Naan. Mint Lime Cooler. As I reached for the Butter Chicken, a different dish caught my attention.

Singapore Noodles with Paneer Gravy. The *exact* thing Jennifer always orders. And then, She walked in. White dress. Effortlessly graceful. I was already in *Cloud 5625*.

"Happy Birthday, Aaron!" A hug. Gucci Bamboo perfume. All over me.

Hamshad pinched me back to reality.

"Thank you, Jennifer."

"May all your dreams come true this year!"

"Really? All my dreams?"

She smiled. *"I don't know. Keep trying. They might come true."* A blush. A gift in my hand.

She took a seat next to Seby. I was floating. Absolutely floating. And that's when my *so-called* friends did what friends do best—ruined it. Mandeep smirked.

"Don't eat the chick, eat the chicken."

I nearly choked.

Halfway through the meal, my father decided to *drop in* on our conversation.

"So, *how's work going for everyone?*"

Hamshad, ever the overachiever answered first.

"*Marvelous! We never imagined we'd get a job like this.*"

Seby nodded. "*Yeah, everything is going well for us.*"

Gilbert, being the brutally honest guy he was, leaned back and said loudly:

"*Please don't lie. They should know the truth.*"

Dad's eyes sharpened. "*Should I be worried?*"

Gilbert grinned.

"*No, uncle. But there was this incident four months ago… and no one has figured out how or why it happened.*"

Silence. All eyes turned toward him. And just like that my birthday party took an unexpected turn.

Chapter 3

Four Months Ago...

Nearly two and a half months had passed since we joined the company, and by now, the team had started to warm up to Gilbert and me. They were nice especially Gopal Varma, the senior-most member, who was widely expected to be the next team leader. But until that day came, we had to endure the wrath of the current team lead: Kailash, a.k.a. *"Mad Dog."*

He was relentless. He *loved* making our lives difficult.

"How's everything going for you all?" I asked, half-expecting everyone to launch into their own set of workplace miseries.

But Jennifer, ever the optimist, smiled. *"Our team leader, Akshaya, is a sweetheart. She's so supportive, never raises her voice, at least not yet."*

Lucky them.

"Great! Let's go out for dinner?" I asked, directing the question toward Jennifer. But, of course, my *so-called* friends took it as an open invitation.

So much for *one-on-one* time.

The elevator ride down was an experience in itself. The air inside felt like ice, but my heart? It was *burning*. Jennifer was standing beside me, her hand lightly brushing against mine. Goosebumps spread across my skin. *"God, if you exist, just give us a power cut. Let the elevator stall for a few minutes. Just me and her."*

No such luck. The doors slid open, and we stepped out into the lobby, heading toward the exit glass doors, the boundary between our 16-story corporate jail and the outside world. And that's when it happened.

A deafening *thud*. A spray of red. A moment of silence so absolute, it drowned out all sound.

For a full minute, my body refused to process what my eyes were seeing. The blood. The shattered bones. Then, it hit me. It was Gopal Varma.

The man who had been our strongest support in the team, reduced to nothing in mere seconds.

The transition from "Gopal Varma" to "the corpse" happened almost instantly. People gathered, whispering in hushed, horrified voices. And within ten minutes, the patrol vehicle arrived.

Meanwhile, social media was already on fire. Facebook. WhatsApp. Instagram. Twitter - oh, sorry, X.

Posts flooded in:

- *"OMG! Someone just jumped from my office building!!"*

- *"Suicide at Care All Tech! IT pressure is too much!!!"*

- *"RIP Gopal. Life is short, guys. Be happy."*

I sighed. It's ridiculous. People post their entire lives online, "Going to work," "Bought an iPhone," "Salary credited," not realizing how easy it makes things for hackers. Now, the *Cyber Artists* had their next masterpiece.

Yet, the police, who had just arrived at the scene were scrambling to clear the crowd. Not to protect evidence, but to prevent traffic congestion on social media.

"What happened? Excuse me! I'm talking to you!" A sharp tap on my shoulder snapped me back to reality.

"We were going for dinner, and he fell in front of us. Is he... dead?"

The officer's voice was grim. *"Yes, he is. But I need to know did someone push him? Or did he jump?"*

Mandeep, still in shock, snapped. *"How the hell are we supposed to know that? Can't you see we have blood all over us? Do we look okay to you?"*

The inspector's jaw tightened. *"Does that mean I shouldn't ask you anything? We need statements from the first witnesses. It's protocol."*

Before his frustration could escalate, a constable rushed over, whispering something in his ear and handing him a polythene bag. The inspector's expression darkened.

Suddenly, the investigation took a different turn. *"Clear the crowd. Everyone leave. Now."* Just like that, we were dismissed.

That night, the office shut down early around 11:30 PM. I rode my bike home on autopilot, my brain too occupied with the Gopal Varma incident to focus on the road.

I kept replaying everything in my mind. He had always been kind. Encouraging. When Kailash first humiliated me at work and I was on the verge of sending a *"I QUIT! F** OFF!"** email, it was Gopal who stopped me.

"I made that mistake once, Aaron. Look where it got me, five years in the same chair, barely making ends meet. Don't let anger decide your future."

And yet, despite his wisdom, he was gone in an instant. By the time I reached home, it was 11:57 PM and I had already washed off the blood at the office. Rebecca, my mother was half-asleep. I slipped past her, straight to my room after opening the house with the spare key I used to carry.

I stared at the ceiling, eyes wide open. I had no idea when sleep finally took over.

The Next Day...

We follow a pattern in life. We see breaking news, talk about it for a week, then move on to the next tragedy.

Gopal Varma's suicide was now the hot topic. His seat next to me was empty. I sighed, unloading my bag. If you reach the office early, there's an unspoken ritual:

- Go to the cafeteria.
- Have coffee/tea.
- Smoke.
- Return exactly at login time.

I turned to leave for the cafeteria, but something made me pause.

A glimpse of the inspector and the constable, exiting the manager's office. In the inspector's hand? A laptop bag. But the shape... it didn't look like a laptop. I let them leave before heading to the cafeteria, where a surprise awaited me, my entire group was already there.

I smirked. *"Mandeep? Am I dreaming? You're here before 6 PM?"*

Yawning, Mandeep groaned. *"Certainly not."*

"All of you came early? Even you, Mandeep? This is historic."

Gilbert, visibly exhausted, muttered, *"No sleep. My ears are still hearing that sound on repeat. So I came early. Any more questions?"*

Fair enough.

Hamshad, never one to stay silent, broke the tension. *"We're all dealing with trauma. We should distract ourselves."*

Seby, ever the sceptic, asked, *"And how do you suggest we do that?"*

"Simple. We have three days off this weekend. Let's go on a trip, Goa? Ooty? Kerala?"

For the first time in 24 hours, I saw smiles returning to their faces. But deep inside, I couldn't move on. Because there was something I saw that night. Something I wasn't ready to talk about.

Chapter 4

Birthday Celebration...

"Aaron, what are they talking about? Is it really true?" My father's voice was thick with agitation.

"Yes, Dad," I said, keeping my tone as calm as possible. "But you don't have to worry about it."

"Really?" He scoffed. "After everything Gilbert just told us, you still think I shouldn't worry about you working in an unsafe place?"

Mandeep, always quick to smooth things over, jumped in. "Uncle, there's no need to be concerned. The police conducted a full investigation. Gopal sir took his own life because of financial troubles."

Suicide? The information I had gathered over the past two months painted a very different picture. But never mind. This wasn't the time or place to challenge that narrative. There was no point in ruining the peace everyone seemed to have finally settled into.

My father exhaled, rubbing his temples. "Even so, I want all of you to be careful. Don't bottle up your stress. If you have any problems, talk to your parents."

The Colonel had started his lecture again. Before he could gain momentum, I quickly cut in. "Guys! Thanks a lot, this is the best birthday ever."

Hamshad grinned. "Come on, buddy. We're friends. And honestly, I'm just happy that everyone actually showed up for the celebration." With a playful wink, he pulled me into a hug.

Of course, it had been two months since we first started planning our *big* trip. And yet, here we were still stuck in the planning phase. As always, when everyone finally agreed, someone would throw in a last-minute excuse. *Parents won't allow it. Doctor's appointment. No money. Urgent work.* The cycle repeated itself endlessly. Planning a group trip in real life was nothing like the movies. If anything, the Instagram reels were more accurate, the ones that said *"Group Trip Planning Be Like..."*

Mandeep, still chewing, groaned. "Can we all shut up and finish this food before it gets cold?"

For once, he had the most sensible statement of the night.

My gaze flickered to Jennifer, and for a moment, our eyes met. A small, knowing smile passed between us before I pointed to her plate. "Mind sharing some of those Singapore Noodles?"

We finished our meal, not a single dish going to waste, and made our way outside.

Jennifer stepped forward, extending her hand to wish me once more, but before I could respond, my parents appeared beside me, and the moment slipped away.

Seby and Jennifer waved as they walked toward their car. "See you at the office."

As we watched them leave, Gilbert turned to me. "Are you mad at me for telling your parents about the incident?"

"No, Gilbert. They should know. It's fine," I reassured him.

He smiled, then pulled me into a hug. "Happy Birthday, buddy! Now get to the office soon, or you're going to get fried on your special day."

The incident had changed Gilbert a lot. He was never the type to ask, *Are you okay? What's going on?* and he certainly wasn't the *caring* type. But now? He did all of it. He had grown closer to everyone, building stronger relationships in ways I never expected.

Small things have a big impact. Life is all about the changes we go through. And as Gilbert reminded me, it was best not to be late for work.

Chapter 5

What We Expect Never Happens. What We Don't Expect Always Does.

Just like that, I was late to the office - twenty minutes late, to be precise. And now, the *Mad Dog* was going to ruin my entire day.

Oh, sorry, *Mad Dog* is our team leader. It doesn't matter if you're a man or woman, single or married, divorced or widowed, stressed or happy he will grind you down to the core with his words. The team had a revolving door of resignations and new hires, and he was one of the main reasons. But if you looked at the bright side, at least the unemployed found a job, and the employed found a better one.

I swiped my ID card at the entrance, the small dog tag around my neck deciding my fate whether the office doors would open or not. As I stepped onto the floor, I scanned my surroundings like a detective, checking if *Mad*

Dog was lurking nearby. A sigh of relief escaped me, he was nowhere to be seen. No immediate bite marks today. I slid into my seat, turned on my computer, and prepared for a normal day.

But then, *a heavy breath behind me.*

I turned slowly.

There he was. The *Mad Dog* had sniffed me out.

"Why do you even bother coming to the office?" His voice dripped with irritation.

I gulped. "I'm really sorry, Kailash. I stayed up late because of my birthday party."

"Oh! I see." His lips curled into a mock smile. "Happy Birthday, Aaron."

"Thank you, Kailash."

His expression darkened. "What the hell? Whether you celebrate or not isn't my concern. Work is my first priority. If you start slacking now, you'll regret it later. You're new here, but your behaviour already says a lot about you."

This was the same old lecture every company had. *You're new and already... You've been here for years, yet... You're the most experienced, so how could you... At your position, how can you...* All I could do was stand there, letting his words wash over me. three minutes and twenty-eight seconds of public humiliation later, he finally wrapped up.

"Get back to work. No compromises in production. Stay an extra twenty minutes today."

"Yes, Kailash," I muttered.

All that ranting, and in the end, all he wanted was for me to stay late. Three minutes wasted. I went to my desk, put my head down, and transformed into a robot for the next few hours. Time passed.

Then, a message popped up on my screen.

"Come over to the canteen. Need to talk to you personally." Jennifer.

In an instant, my mind spiralled into overdrive. *Love? confession? Marriage? Kids? Growing old together? Dying in each other's arms?*

I snapped out of my daydream and replied immediately.

"Will be there in two minutes."

The office canteen was our usual spot, a place for overpriced *chai* that was basically sugary brown water and ten-rupee Maggi noodles being sold for fifty. But today, the canteen felt different, like something straight out of Torres del Paine National Park.

And there, at the centre, stood Jennifer in an angelic white dress.

"Jennifer?" I gasped, trying to catch my breath.

"Hey, Aaron! Why are you panting?"

"Lift wasn't working… took the stairs."

"Oh! Okay." She smiled and held out something to me. "I wanted to give this to you."

A golden card. I flipped it over, my eyes scanning the text.

"Joel weds Jennifer." My heart stopped.

"Wow…" I forced out a laugh. "Only three weeks left until your wedding?"

She nodded. "Yes. He works in France, and he's coming to India on vacation. We're getting married while he's here."

I felt a familiar sting in my eyes, tears threatening to fall. But before I could process it, our gang stormed into the canteen, crashing our private moment.

I turned to Jennifer. "Did you call them here?"

"Of course! They're my friends too. I need to invite them to my wedding."

"What's happening here?" Mandeep asked, looking between us. "Did we miss something important?"

Jennifer beamed. "I'm getting married in three weeks, and my best gang has to be there to make the occasion special!"

Laughter, hugs, and congratulations filled the air. Everyone celebrated.

Except me.

I simply stood there, staring at the invitation, my mind detached from the moment. Finally, I handed the card to Gilbert and forced a smile. "Okay, everyone, I already have to extend my shift by twenty minutes. Can't afford to waste any more time. Congratulations, Jennifer. Have a wonderful life."

Without another word, I left the canteen.

I made my way to the men's restroom, shutting myself inside. A moment later, Hamshad, Mandeep, and Gilbert followed. They saw the tears before I could even wipe them away.

Mandeep, usually the funny one, grew serious. "Forget it, Aary. One day, she'll realize."

I shook my head. "You think love is about waiting for someone to 'realize'?" My voice was tight, but firm. "Love is about standing by them, staying with them, thinking about them, wanting them to be happy, whether they're with you or not."

Mandeep fell silent. "Sorry, Aary."

"If you love her this much, why don't you tell her?" Hamshad asked, his voice steady.

The room grew quiet.

What people often forgot was that the walls between the men's and women's restrooms were *thin*.

On the other side, Jennifer and Seby had heard *everything*.

I took a deep breath.

"Yes, I love her," I admitted. "I love her so much… but I never told her. I never wanted to lose a friend while searching for a lover inside her."

Hamshad whispered, "Aary…"

I straightened up.

And then, I *shouted*.

"I LOVE YOU, JENNIFER! I KNOW YOU'RE THERE! MEET ME IN THE CANTEEN IN FIVE MINUTES!"

Jennifer, standing frozen on the other side of the wall, stared at Seby, her mind racing. "How the hell did he know I was here?"

Still processing what had just happened, she rushed into the lift and pressed the button for the ninth floor. The doors opened. Jennifer stepped out, her gaze locking onto mine.

"How did you know I was there?" she demanded.

I smiled. "I love you."

"Oh, is that so?" She folded her arms. "Well, I'm getting married in three weeks."

"I know, Jennifer." My smile widened.

She frowned. "Why are you laughing? And you still haven't answered my question. Stop laughing. It's annoying."

I chuckled. "At first, I didn't pay much attention to the invitation. But when I looked at it properly in the restroom as Mandeep dropped it beside me, I noticed a few things. First: *Joel, son of Muniyandi and Kannamma,* weird. Second: *Hogwarts School of Wizards, France?* Even weirder. And the best part? The printer's mark on the back: *Single Copy Only.*"

Jennifer's lips parted slightly.

"You printed just one invitation," I continued. "And you gave it to me. That's when I knew."

She stared at me, stunned. "You're really a cop material."

I took a step closer. "Jennifer, you still haven't answered my proposal."

She let out a small sigh before smiling. "I don't love you, Aaron. But you'll always have me as a friend for life."

Our gang burst into the canteen, cheering. The celebration resumed, and we laughed over overpriced *chai* and Maggi. Happiness radiated from every face. None of us knew... That it wouldn't last. That soon, everything would change. Forever.

Chapter 6

"Love is a beautiful feeling." We've all heard this countless times. But to me, that statement is incomplete. Love isn't just about the tender moments: caring, hugging, supporting, kissing, messaging, calling, admiring, and making love. Yes, those are the beautiful parts. But what about the arguments, the disagreements, the misunderstandings? What about possessiveness, the suffocation from a lack of personal space, and the moments where it feels like you're losing yourself?

Love is like holding a knife by the blade: hold it too tight, and you'll bleed; hold it too loose, and you'll drop it; hold it just right, and you'll remain unharmed.

There were days we loved like crazy, and there were days we drove each other to the edge. But no matter what, we never let go. Like every other couple, we strolled through parks, visited beaches, shopped at malls, and went to the movies sometimes just the two of us, sometimes with our gang.

One particular incident stands out in our memories. We had planned to watch *Jawan* over the weekend, and, as usual, I was on time, waiting for the latecomers including Jennifer. Just then, a loud commotion erupted in the parking lot. A crowd had gathered, shouting and pushing. As responsible citizens, it's our duty to investigate.

A short man was being beaten mercilessly. I never liked the word *dwarf* being used to describe someone, but unfortunately, society does.

I stepped in. "Why are you hitting him? What did he do?"

Someone from the crowd shouted, "He stole a lady's purse!"

"Fine. If you think he's guilty, take him to the police. No one has the right to beat another human being. Who's willing to file a complaint?"

Suddenly, silence. We really need to applaud these people, they had followed their childhood lessons religiously. *Unity is strength!* They stood together to beat someone but not to take responsibility.

"If you're not filing a complaint, just take the bag and leave," I said.

The man, blood dripping from his cheek, looked at me. "Thank you, sir."

"What's your name?"

"Reva. You come to Keelaveethi and ask for me; they'll bring you straight to me."

"Why do you steal?" I asked, genuinely curious.

"Looting runs in our blood, generation after generation. It's not easy to change. But you helped me, so I owe you one. Take my number. If you ever need help, call me."

I don't know why, but I noted his number down.

A few minutes later, my angel arrived, slipping her hand into mine. I led her inside, taking our usual corner seats. In the darkness, I had hopes of creating my own little *kissing scene.*

The Interval Incident

During the break, we stepped out to grab some popcorn and Coke, *normal* popcorn, not the overpriced caramel one. Out of nowhere, Seby ran up to us, crying.

Hamshad was the first to ask, "What happened, Seby? Why are you crying?"

Tears streamed down her face. "I got a message saying Rs. 20,000 has been deducted from my bank account! That was for my EMI. I don't even know how it happened!"

Panic settled in. We huddled together, trying to think of a way to retrieve the money. Meanwhile, our fun-maker, Mandeep, stood there laughing.

"Aary, does anyone here want a donut?" he asked casually.

I turned to him, irritated. "Mandeep, this is serious! Seby lost a lot of money."

He chuckled. "Aary, I bought a messaging system that mimics bank SMS alerts. Just as a prank, I sent her a message. I didn't think she'd panic without checking her actual bank balance."

I stared at him in disbelief. "Mandeep, this is not how you joke with friends! Look at her... she's devastated."

Realizing his mistake, Mandeep muttered, "Sorry, Seby. I didn't mean to scare you."

But the damage was done. Seby turned away and walked back into the theatre, angry and hurt. We shot Mandeep a warning glance, *don't ever pull something like this again.*

In friendship, we share moments of love and laughter, but we also endure the difficult ones. Love had taught me many things, and one of its most important lessons was: *Always look at the brighter side.* Holding relationships together wasn't just about love, it was about resilience.

Rewards & Recognition Event, Next Day...

Excitement buzzed through the office. The half yearly Rewards & Recognition event was about to begin. It started with a solemn tribute—a few moments of silence for Gopal Varma, a colleague who had passed away. Memories of him filled the air, but as with everything in life, it was time to let go and move forward.

The winners were announced one by one, each stepping up to receive a certificate and a ₹2,500 Amazon gift card.

Rewards & Recognition? More like *Repeat & Recapture*. These events were just corporate strategies to push employees harder, making them work more and live less. I overheard someone say they had won three years in a row. By now, he had probably forgotten what his wife looked like. And if he went home and had sex, he was likely thinking about the next day's workload instead. (*The only upside? He wouldn't finish too quickly.*)

In our group, we had one such workaholic, and we were eagerly waiting for his name to be called.

"And the Best Performer for the Kenver Project goes to… Gilbert!"

The moment his name was announced, we erupted into cheers so loud that the entire room turned to stare at us. But we didn't care. Our friend had won, and we were going to celebrate it.

Because that's what love and friendship are all about—being there for each other, in success, in failure, in laughter, and in tears.

Chapter 7

5 Weeks Ago...

We never truly know how a bad day can turn our lives upside down.

Kailash was already barking at everyone. When he was in this kind of mood, no amount of reasoning would get through to him. A mad dog at his peak, he suddenly noticed my empty seat and gestured for Gilbert to approach him.

"Where is your friend?"

"I really don't know, Kailash. He didn't say anything to me."

"You guys roam together, fetch water together, go to the restroom together, but you don't know whether he took leave or not? You gays defend each other well."

"Kailash!!!"

"Go outside, take your phone, call your boyfriend, and tell him he needs to be in the office within half an hour."

Fuming with anger and irritation, Gilbert stormed out to the locker room, grabbed his Nokia 8210, and kept calling me until I finally picked up.

"Hello!!"

"Aaron, where the hell are you?"

"I'm not feeling well. I came to the hospital."

"You didn't inform Kailash? Come on, Aaron! He's been shouting, and the words he threw at me were hard to take. He insists you come within half an hour."

"Gilbert!! Are you serious? I just told you I'm sick, waiting for treatment, and you're asking me to come to the office? We are not slaves. Kailash won't understand because of who he is, but you're my friend. Even you don't understand?"

"I'm sorry, Aaron. His words were too ugly. You take care and go home. I'll meet you tomorrow."

"It's okay. I'll call you later. Bye."

Morning 03:30 AM...

A sudden knock on the door, accompanied by the ringing bell, startled the house. Colonel walked toward the door, rifle in hand, and opened it. My friends, scared by the sight of the weapon, hesitated, but his hands lowered the rifle as he welcomed them in.

"What are you all doing here at this hour?"

"We came to see the patient," Mandeep said in his usual playful tone.

"There's nothing major with him. Sit down, I'll call him."

My half-asleep mother rubbed her eyes and walked into the hall. "Who is it at this time?"

In unison, they all chirped, "Hi, Mom!!"

"Really? What are you guys doing here now?"

Colonel's stern voice cut through, "They've come to see your son since he wasn't feeling well. Prepare some tea and biscuits for them."

I struggled to walk steadily into the hall, but my eyes opened fully when my gang enveloped me in a hug. To be honest, the only hug I truly felt was Jennifer's—I knew who had brought them here.

Jennifer's expression silently asked how I was doing, and I responded with a reassuring glance that I was completely fine.

"Guys, it was just a fever. I would have been back at the office by this evening."

Mom served tea and biscuits as Jennifer softly whined, "Gilbert said you sounded so serious and agitated. After hearing that, I felt like I had to see you."

Mom caught that and glanced at Jennifer, prompting her to quickly rephrase, "Gilbert and everyone felt like seeing you."

Gilbert approached me in a low voice, "How are you, buddy?"

"I'm completely fine, bud. Don't worry. I'm sorry I sounded rude yesterday."

"You were right. I was just pressured by Kailash's words."

"Yes, and now that has caused a lot of problems!" Hamshad said seriously.

"What did you do, Gilbert?" I asked.

Yesterday, Evening...

Still stung by our phone conversation, Gilbert silently returned to his workstation, while Kailash continued yelling at everyone. I honestly couldn't understand how such people even got jobs. Character, behaviour—everything differs from person to person, but this was beyond normal.

"Where is your boyfriend?"

"Kailash, he's not feeling well and won't be coming today."

"Who is he to decide that?"

"Who are you?" Gilbert's loud voice silenced the floor.

"What did you just do?"

"I work for the company, not for you. Do you think we are slaves, expected to tolerate your disrespect silently? I have a designation, and I do my work accordingly. You have a designation, so do yours. This is not a jail, and you are certainly not a jailer. Show some respect to everyone on this team."

Taken aback, Kailash, now aware that all eyes were on him, coldly responded, "Sit down, Gilbert. We will discuss this tomorrow." His expression was a mix of anger, rage, and revenge. Kailash didn't care if someone was rich or poor; if he wanted you out, he'd do everything in his power to make it happen.

Present Moment...

Shocked by the revelation, I reacted, "What have you done, Gilbert?"

"I had no choice. Either I endured disrespect, or I stood up for myself. I chose the second option."

"But this will impact your career. You're the only one earning, did you forget that?"

"I didn't forget. The only thing I forgot was self-respect."

"Your mom worked so hard to get you here, Gilly."

"Do you think I don't care? You don't know the worst part… Kailash called me a bastard."

Silence filled the room as he looked at me with accusing eyes.

"I'm sorry, Gilly. I didn't know."

"It's not your fault. My damn father, who abandoned me when I was five, is responsible for all this criticism and pain."

Gilbert was overwhelmed with emotion. We had never seen him like this before. Words and stress can cut deeper than a knife. We all sat there, dumbfounded. Gilbert grabbed his bag and walked out, despite Mandeep's attempt to stop him.

Breaking the silence, Mandeep sighed, "I think this urgent meeting turned into a disaster. It's fine; he'll be in the office this evening, and we'll talk to him then. Don't worry, guys. Cheer up and have your tea."

It wasn't the farewell we had expected. Everyone stood up and conveyed their care before leaving. Jennifer looked at me, but I avoided her gaze, my mind occupied with everything that had happened. My mother, ever observant, noticed both my stress and Jennifer's longing glance.

"Jennifer, how are you getting home?" Mom asked.

"I'll book a cab, Aunty."

"Aaron, go drop her."

"Mom??"

"Go. It's not safe for her to go alone."

My rare sight of my parents agreeing on something. Excited yet nervous, I started my bike. Jennifer climbed on without touching me, keeping a solid two-kilometre gap as if to punish me.

"Jennifer, I know you're angry. I'm sorry."

Silence.

"Jeni, I was just shocked about everything with Gilbert."

"You should've loved Gilbert instead of me."

"Come on! He's my school friend."

"Stop at the next corner. I'll walk from here."

I parked in a dimly lit spot, and as she got off, I grabbed her hand, pulling her in for a kiss.

"Apology not accepted."

Wrapping my arms around her waist, I whispered, "How else should I apologize?"

"Not now, but after marriage, it will be harder."

"I want to know how."

"Only after marriage. Now get lost."

I left in a half heart and mind thinking of the horror that is about to take over this evening.

Chapter 8

Evening 5:30 PM…

I parked my bike so fast that my gang immediately noticed something was wrong. I was disturbed deeply. Every day, I used to pick up Gilbert on my way to the office, but today, he didn't even wait for me. As I walked quickly towards the entrance, Hamshad and Jennifer intercepted me.

"Are you heading for a race?" Jennifer asked, her expression reminding me of our morning conversation.

"No," I muttered. "I usually pick up Gilbert, but his mother said he left for the office around 4 PM."

Hamshad, in his usual calming tone, said, "Okay, relax, buddy. Maybe he had some pending work from yesterday."

"Or?" I asked, my mind already racing to worst-case scenarios.

"Or what do you mean?"

"We'll find out as soon as we reach the floor."

We had two elevators for the ten-story building. I pressed the button so hard and repeatedly that people around me started staring. As soon as the elevator arrived, we got in, but the stops on each floor felt agonizingly slow. When we finally reached our floor, I was so restless that I forgot my usual routine placing my bag and mobile in the locker. Instead, I rushed inside.

There he was, Gilbert, walking towards me with an envelope in his hand.

"What happened? Why did you come in so early?" I asked.

He held up the envelope. "I got a call from the office this afternoon and came in to get this."

"What is this?"

"My termination letter. Gilbert, that's me, has been terminated due to misconduct on the floor."

"They need to conduct an inquiry before taking such decisions."

"That's for people with recommendations and referrals. Not for me."

"You stay here. I'll talk to the head. Please don't leave."

Adrenaline surged through me. My mind completely shut out the morning's self-reminders to stay out of trouble. I was already running towards the Delivery Head's office.

Without knocking, I stormed inside. "How can you terminate an employee without any inquiry? We'll raise a complaint!"

I was speaking to the back of his rolling chair. Slowly, he turned around—his expression cold, his eyes filled with malice. "Complaint?" He chuckled. "Go ahead. Your friend already signed the document, accepting his misconduct. No complaint can change that."

"Sir, this isn't protocol. A formal inquiry with a four-member committee must be conducted before taking action."

"Everything was verified," he said, smirking. "Not a single employee spoke up in his defence. And call me Melvin, not Sir."

"I'm here to say it."

"You weren't even present yesterday," he snapped. "Cut the nonsense, Aaron. The formalities are completed. Now excuse me, I have a meeting."

My heart was pounding. My fists clenched. I wanted to land one straight on his smug face, knock out a tooth, at least one. But before I could act, my team leader entered the room and dragged me outside.

"What do you think you're doing?"

Furious, I shot back, "It's because of you he lost his job! He's the first in his family to get a white-collar job, and you destroyed his career. Why did you do it?"

I lunged at him, grabbing his collar, but Hamshad, Mandeep, Jennifer, and a few others restrained me, pulling me out of the floor.

I ran downstairs, searching for Gilbert, but he was gone. Jennifer followed me as I frantically looked around. She called my name, but I didn't respond. Finally, I reached my bike, ready to search for him elsewhere.

"If you won't listen, go to hell!" Jennifer shouted. "Are you ready to lose me as well?"

I got off my bike, frustration boiling over. "Do you even hear yourself? He's the only person earning for his family!"

"You think I don't know that?" she snapped. "You're thinking for him, but did he think for himself?"

"What are you saying?"

"He didn't fight for his job. He didn't even try to hold his ground to feed his family. And in the end, he didn't even wait for you."

Her words hit like a slap. She was right.

"Corporate companies feed off their employees," she continued. "They don't care if you live or die. If you want a job in today's world, you have to adapt to this disrespectful culture. Team leaders will yell at you, managers won't recognize your efforts, they'll tell you you're unfit for even a BPO job, even with an engineering degree. Politics and corporate politics are the same: those in power do whatever they want, and no one can question them. Understand that! If you still want to throw away your job and me for a meaningless fight, go ahead!"

I sank to my knees, tears streaming down my face. Jennifer knelt beside me and hugged me.

Don't get me wrong, but I've seen how this world works. People wake up at 6:30 AM, hit the gym, take a walk in the park, or use that extra hour for sleep. Some eat breakfast, others skip it calling it a diet or blaming their busy schedules. By 8:30 or 9:00 AM, most of us transform into robots. We cram into cabs, buses, or trains, or ride bikes to reach ten- to fifteen-story fingerprint-accessible prisons. We sit in cushioned chairs, stare at 29cm tall screens, and try to change a 510.1-million square km planet. After a long day, filled with unlimited free tea and coffee, we go home, mindlessly scroll through reels, feeds, or watch TV, then sleep.

What kind of life is this? This is the life of a corporate slave.

One of the most painful things in the world: being forced by your own mind to do things you don't want to do. The mind refuses to listen to the heart, and the heart refuses to listen to the mind.

Chapter 9

Three Weeks and Three Days Ago…

Studies suggest that it takes nearly a year to recover from the grieving process after a loss. Ever since Gilbert left, the controller of our group was gone. He was the one who kept us on track, reminding us if our breaks ran too long, pushing us to meet deadlines, ensuring we stayed focused. Without him, that structure was missing.

Breaks weren't the same anymore. Conversations had become scarce, and even Mandeep's usual jokes failed to spark laughter among us.

Hamshad, Mandeep, and Jennifer kept a close watch on me, knowing I had taken Gilbert's departure the hardest. I had developed a habit of disappearing during breaks, wandering off to the canteen alone.

One such evening, as I sipped tea by myself, I noticed someone rushing toward me, shoving chairs aside, panting heavily. It was Mandeep.

"What happened? You're gasping like you just ran a marathon. Sit down, have some water."

With heavy breaths and frantic hand gestures signalling 'no,' he managed to blurt out, "There's a problem. You shouldn't stay here. We need to leave now."

I frowned. "What are you blabbering about? Did you have a bad dream or something?"

Ignoring my scepticism, he frantically searched behind the canteen TV for the remote, tapped it to adjust the batteries, and switched to an English news channel. On the screen, I saw him, the company's head, the same man I had confronted two weeks ago was addressing the press.

"Please remain silent. I will answer all your questions after my statement."

The reporters obediently took their seats, eager to hear his explanation.

"It has come to our attention that nearly 200 patient records from Kenver Cancer Care Institute in Indiana, USA, have been leaked. This breach has caused severe consequences, including an outrageous attack on the institute, one that resulted in the tragic death of a doctor. We are ashamed as an organization because the leak originated from within our company.

Following an internal investigation, we have verified through CCTV footage and digital records that this reckless act was committed by Aaron Wyatt, a new joiner who has been with the organization for just over five months.

His motive? Anger, stemming from his friend's termination four weeks prior. As a result, necessary legal action is being taken. The Indian Police Force, along with the Central Bureau of Investigation, has begun proceedings to extradite him for trial at the International Court of Justice.

Additionally, we are already working with cybercrime specialists and the affected institute to ensure that all leaked data is erased from the digital sphere. As an organization, we deeply regret the distress caused to the affected patients and their families."

My body went rigid. The words echoed in my mind, but I struggled to process them. I sat frozen, paralyzed by shock.

Mandeep quickly muted the TV and grabbed me by the shoulders, shaking me hard. "Aary, snap out of it! We need to go. Right now!"

But I couldn't move.

Realizing my daze, he seized my wrist firmly and pulled me along with him. We made our way to the elevator, intending to slip out unnoticed.

Too late.

As soon as the doors slid open, uniformed officers stepped out, handcuffs at the ready.

"Mr. Aaron Wyatt?" one of them asked.

Before I could respond, cold metal snapped around my wrists. The grip was firm, unyielding. Murmurs spread like wildfire. Employees gathered, watching in stunned silence as I was dragged through the office.

Bright camera flashes blinded me, reporters pushing forward to capture the best angle of my humiliation.

Within moments, I was shoved into the back of a patrol vehicle, the doors slamming shut behind me.

Shocked. Humiliated. Enraged.

I sat there in silence, bracing myself for what awaited me next.

Chapter 10

Hamshad, Mandeep, Jennifer, and Seby were shaken by the incident. They tried to leave the company through the front gate but hesitated, knowing the reporters outside would bombard them with questions. Realizing the implications, they decided to exit through the back gate. As soon as a cab arrived, they rushed to my house, ready to deliver the shocking news to my parents. My arrest had taken place at 1:30 AM, and there was no way my parents would have been awake, watching an English news channel to learn about it. At 3:30 AM, my gang was banging on our door.

The relentless knocking startled my parents awake. My father opened the door with my mother right behind him, both confused and groggy. The moment they heard what had happened, they sprang into action, not with fainting spells or heart attacks like in movies, but with swift determination. They gathered whatever essentials they needed to rush to the police station. Just as they were about to leave, a man appeared in the doorway.

Everyone tensed up, fearing that the media had followed them. My father, his voice rigid but tinged with fear, demanded, "Who are you? What do you want?"

Hamshad, tense with anxiety, snapped, "Are you from the media? Leave us alone! We're already in deep trouble."

The man stepped into the hall and spoke calmly. "I am a lawyer appointed by the government to represent Aaron Wyatt in this case. My name is Vignesh Aacharya."

My mother exhaled a breath of relief. "Please, save my son. He has never harmed anyone, nor would he commit such a crime."

"I need to speak with him first. Let's go to the station and discuss the rest there," Aacharya responded.

During the COVID-19 lockdown, 55% of people feared police brutality, according to online reports. I had always wondered why innocent people would fear the police. Now, I understood.

The moment I entered the station, I was met with a brutal slap across my face. No questions, no investigation, just an immediate presumption of guilt. The officers didn't ask me *if* I had leaked the information; they only demanded to know *how* I did it. Every refusal to speak earned me another slap, my cheeks turning pink with each strike. Boot marks imprinted my back as I endured the beating in silence.

When my parents, my friends, and the lawyer arrived, they found me shirtless, my skin bearing the marks of police 'interrogation.' My mother screamed, "Oh my God! What have they done to you?"

"Silence!" barked a constable.

My father, for the first time in his life, spoke to me gently. "Aaron, don't worry. We will fight this. He is the lawyer who will represent you."

Jennifer, tears streaming down her face, couldn't speak. The lawyer signalled everyone to step back and whispered to me, "I know you're innocent. Tell me everything, from three weeks ago until now." While I recounted the events, Aacharya subtly slipped a key and a small note into my hand. I took it without drawing attention.

Once my story was finished, he leaned in. "Stay strong."

The inspector stormed in, yelling, "Enough! Everyone out!" My family and friends were forcibly removed. As Jennifer was being pulled away, I locked eyes with her, silently assuring her that I would be okay.

In the cell, I moved to a blind spot to read the note. *Jump to see us. Government Hospital. Waiting.* I examined the key, it was for the handcuffs.

A police cell is nothing like what you see in movies. The walls were so stained that I couldn't tell if they were originally white or brown. Bloodstains from past beatings remained uncleaned. The stench of urine was unbearable. I sat in the least filthy corner, refusing to close my eyes for even a second.

At 9:30 AM, the inspector stomped into the cell and yanked me to my feet. Without fresh clothes, without even brushing my teeth, I was cuffed and stuffed into a police van. I had the key hidden in my palm, waiting for the right moment.

The van was a rusting relic from the 1980s. There were only two officers, one driving and one seated next to me. A commotion erupted outside, a staged fight meant to create a distraction. The officer riding with me turned his head, giving me the split second I needed.

I swiftly unlocked the cuffs and tossed them toward him. As he flinched, I grabbed his gun and held it to his head. "Stay still," I growled. Without hesitation, I leaped from the moving van and sprinted toward the waiting ambulance.

If I had a stopwatch, I might have beaten Wayde van Niekerk's 400m world record. I dodged through the chaotic hospital entrance, where the lawyer was waiting. The moment I jumped into the ambulance, the sirens blared, and we sped away.

The lawyer dropped me at a safe house. He gave me a thumbs-up before leaving. I stepped inside, cleaned myself up, and sat motionless, my mind racing.

I needed answers. The company's administrator, Shylesh, was the only person who could verify digital imprints and CCTV footage. He was also a close friend of Gilbert. Without hesitation, I picked up a new burner phone and dialled his number.

"Hello? Gilbert?"

A cautious voice responded, "Yes. Who is this?"

"It's me, Aaron."

A gasp. "Aaron! Where are you? The police are looking for you everywhere. You're all over the news! You need to surrender."

"I can't. They're framing me. I need your help."

"How?"

"Not over the phone. Meet me at Velachery Electric Railway Station tomorrow at 1:00 PM."

"If they catch me with you, I'm finished."

"Trust me. There won't be any problems." I hung up.

My life had flipped overnight. Three weeks ago, Gilbert was fired. Now, I was a fugitive. A false accusation, a brutal night in police custody, my family and friends suffering because of me. Tomorrow would mark the beginning of my fight for the truth.

But first, I needed to rest. The road ahead was long.

Chapter 11

The plan was flawless. Gilbert stood amidst the bustling crowd at the railway station, his eyes darting around in search of me. It was the first-ever Airshow in Chennai, and the entire city was converging toward Marina Beach, the second-longest urban beach in the world. Trains were packed, the air thick with excitement and chatter. But amidst all this, danger lurked.

I grabbed Gilbert's wrist and whispered, "Come with me. Don't let go."

"Aary, what the hell is going on?" he asked, confused but obedient.

"We're being followed. We need to disappear now."

The sheer volume of people made it impossible for anyone to make a move without drawing attention. If panic broke out, chaos would ensue. That was my advantage. I maneuverer us through the crowd with calculated precision, slipping past commuters, ducking behind vendors, using every blind spot to my favour. Then, a sharp tug, someone had grabbed my shirt. With a forceful yank, I tore free, leaving them clutching a ripped piece of fabric.

We broke away from the station, the police officers left searching, baffled by our sudden vanishing act. We sprinted through narrow alleys until we reached an abandoned house nearby. Gasping for breath, Gilbert turned to me, his face etched with fear and anger.

"Aaron, what are you even doing? Do you think you can just outrun this? They aren't going to forget or forgive!"

I locked eyes with him, deadly serious. "Gilbert, I have no choice. If I don't prove my innocence, my life is over. I need your help. Are you in or not?" I paused. "If you can't do this, I'll find another way."

He exhaled sharply, rubbing his temple. "I'm not saying no, Aary. I just... this is a lot. What do you need?"

"First, give me your phone."

He hesitated but handed it over. I switched it off and returned it to him. "Don't turn it on until we're done. They'll track you."

"Fine. Now what?"

"Melvin announced in the press meet that CCTV footage and digital imprints confirmed my involvement. Only one person could've handled that—Shylesh, our administrator."

"So?"

"I need to meet him."

Gilbert paled. "Aary, you're taking an insane risk. Are you sure?"

I nodded. "More than ever. We're going to XOXO Hostel."

He frowned. "How do you know he stays there?"

"Because you told Mandeep about it when he was looking for a room. Remember?"

"Shit. My bad memory."

"You lead the way. I'll get the truth out of him."

I pulled a cap over my head, adjusted my face mask, and we hailed an auto. Gilbert gave the driver the destination. As we drove through the city, I knew Gilbert's doubts were valid. If Shylesh refused to talk, I had no Plan B. And if I were in Gilbert's shoes, would I be helping a fugitive? Probably not. Yet, here he was.

We reached the hostel, a typical run-down place with no CCTV—just a warden who acted as one but barely functioned. That worked in our favour. We entered undetected, reaching Shylesh's locked room. But hostels had a trick, some tenants left spare keys in their shoes for emergencies. A quick check, and bingo, we found it.

Inside, we searched for anything useful, but nothing stood out. Then, outside the window, we spotted him getting dropped off by a bike. No time to think. We switched off the lights and waited.

The door creaked open. Shylesh entered, flicked the light switch. And my fist crashed into his face.

He crumpled to the floor, unconscious. Gilbert and I dragged him to a chair, tying him up and sealing his mouth with tape. A splash of water brought him back, groggy and panicked. His wild eyes darted around the room, locking onto me.

I ripped the tape from his mouth, leaning in close, pressing a pocketknife against his throat. "You answer my questions, you walk out of here. You don't do well, let's not find out."

Gilbert, phone in hand, was already recording.

Shylesh's breath came in short gasps. "W-what do you want to know?"

"Question one: Which CCTV footage did you verify to frame me? Tell the truth, or I swear, you'll regret it."

His face drained of colour. "The... the footage was doctored. You were on a break. We morphed it to make it look like you were at your system."

Gilbert cursed under his breath. I clenched my jaw, keeping my voice steady. "How did you access my system? how did you crack through my password?"

Silence. Shylesh trembled, sweat dripping from his forehead. I leaned in, pressing the knife slightly deeper.

He whimpered, "I—I did it remotely."

My blood boiled. "How did you get my password?"

Before he could answer, a sound cut through the air, police sirens, closing in fast.

"Tell me!" I demanded.

Shylesh's eyes flickered with pure terror. "It... it was Melvin! He ordered me to do it!"

Gilbert yanked me back. "Aaron! We need to leave NOW!"

No time to think. We bolted from the hostel, running until we found a cab. Heart pounding, I slid in, breathless, my mind racing. Gilbert looked at me, shaken.

"Where now?"

I exhaled, my grip tightening. "To the devil's den. We're going to see Melvin."

Chapter 12

We got off the cab. I took the fire exit staircase while Gilbert took the elevator, his face calm, almost too calm. He reached the front desk first, where the receptionist barely looked up.

"I'm here to collect my relieving letter and salary slips from HR."

"Alright, sir. Please have a seat, I'll check with them."

As soon as she stepped away, Gilbert moved swiftly, his fingers brushing across the receptionist's desk. A trainee's ID card was within reach. He grabbed it, swiped it against the access panel, and slipped inside. Now, it was my turn. I lingered near the fire exit door, waiting. Seconds felt like minutes, and then, *click*, the door creaked open from the inside. I slipped through, the air inside thick with the staleness of corporate betrayal.

The office was mostly empty, save for two employees sitting at the far end, engrossed in their overtime work. Gilbert strode ahead while I moved toward Jennifer's desk, my fingers slipping a letter into her drawer, a silent message she would find when it is meant to be.

Then, we reached the room of hell.

Melvin sat with his back to us, his chair slightly tilted, his voice smooth and confident as he spoke into his phone.

"I'll handle it. You don't need to get involved yet."

He turned, and the moment his gaze met mine, his lips curled into a smirk. Not surprised. Not panicked. Just… amused.

"Aaron. I have to say, I didn't expect you to figure it out. And yet, here you are." He chuckled, shaking his head. "I underestimated you."

"Why?" My voice was sharp, cutting through the stale air.

"Why?" He leaned back, exhaling as if the answer was obvious. "Because I don't owe you an explanation. But since you're about to die here or in a U.S. prison, I suppose there's no harm in telling you the truth."

His tone turned casual, almost conversational. "This company? It's just a front. Our *real* business lies elsewhere. It started small, selling patient data to insurance agencies. But that wasn't enough. So we expanded. We started harvesting organs from patients in critical condition, selling them on the black market. And then? We got greedy. Doctors, desperate for money, helped us take organs from *healthy* patients. It was all going smoothly until a certain doctor at Kenver Cancer Care caught wind of our little operation. Six months we tried to shut him up. But he was stubborn. So, we had to solve the problem permanently. A riot. A staged incident. He never saw it coming."

My blood ran cold, but I forced my voice to remain steady. "You still haven't answered my question. Why me?"

He smirked. "It was either you or Gilbert. You both worked for the institute, and we couldn't risk either of you sniffing around."

I clenched my fists. "Kailash tried to warn me, didn't he?"

Melvin laughed. "Poor Kailash. He actually thought you'd leave if he kept pushing you away. He had no idea you were so damn stubborn."

I pulled out my phone. "It's over, Melvin. I have video proof. Your own administrator confessed that you ordered him to doctor the CCTV footage and access my system remotely."

Melvin's smirk didn't fade. Instead, it widened. "Do you, now?"

His gaze shifted. My stomach twisted as I turned. Gilbert stepped forward, my phone in his hand. He wasn't giving it to *me*.

"What... Gilbert?" My voice was hoarse.

Melvin let out a slow, mocking clap. "And *this* is the part where it gets fun."

The air turned suffocating as the realization slammed into me. "It was *you*? You gave them my password?"

Gilbert's lips curled into something that was neither regret nor pride. Just… indifference. "Yeah."

Melvin leaned back. "Kailash tried to save you, but Gilbert? He came straight to *me*. Sold you out before you even knew you were a target."

I turned back to Gilbert, my voice barely above a whisper. "Why?"

His smile widened. "Because you were always ahead of me. School, college, work. Every damn time, you had to be *better*. And Jennifer?" His face darkened. "She was supposed to be mine. But no. She chose *you*."

I felt sick. My so-called best friend. The person I trusted the most.

Melvin sighed dramatically. "Well, this has been fun, but… oh, would you look at that? The police are here."

Sirens wailed in the distance, growing closer.

I looked between the two traitors, their grins etched into my memory like scars. I had two choices: stand here and get caught, or run.

I ran.

Bolting toward the fire exit, I shoved the door open and took the stairs three at a time. The sound of pounding feet behind me sent adrenaline surging through my veins. I couldn't stop. Not now. Not when the game was so close to ending.

I burst out into the open air, gulping in breath after breath as I disappeared into the night.

Present Day...

I sprinted through the darkened streets, my heart hammering in my chest as the shouts of police officers echoed behind me. Sirens blared, slicing through the night like a predator closing in on its prey. My breath was ragged, my body aching from the relentless chase, but my mind was even louder, screaming with unanswered questions.

How do I clear my name?

How do I stop that bastard from running his organ-trafficking empire?

What should I do to Gilbert for stabbing me in the back?

Is there even a way to fix this nightmare?

And the most haunting question of all, *Who the hell was Melvin talking to on the phone when I walked into that office?*

Every part of me burned for vengeance, but first, I needed to survive.

The bridge loomed ahead. Below, the murky waters of the Adyar River churned under the dim city lights. There was no time to hesitate. The pounding footsteps behind me grew louder.

A leap of faith.

I launched myself off the edge.

Whoosh!

The wind roared in my ears as I plunged downward, the icy embrace of the river swallowing me whole. Darkness surrounded me, and for a moment, everything was silent, just me and the weight of the storm I had to face.

And this storm was far from over.

Chapter 13

Police Headquarters, Chennai...

A black SUV tore through the gates of the police headquarters, screeching to a halt at the entrance. The moment the car stopped, a swarm of reporters and flashing cameras surged forward, yelling over each other, desperate for a statement.

The driver's door swung open, and out stepped **DGP Mylvaganan**, the man known for cracking cold cases like they were made of glass. He had only been in office for six weeks, but his reputation preceded him.

Ignoring the barrage of questions, he stormed into the building.

Inside the conference room, a group of high-ranking officers stood at attention as he entered.

"Good morning, Sir!" They saluted in unison.

His glare was sharp enough to cut through steel.

"Stick that good morning up your filthy asses!" he barked, slamming a file onto the table. "An accused has been on the run for three days, and you idiots still haven't caught him? Do you even feel ashamed wearing that uniform?"

A tense silence filled the room.

SP Sreejith, a no-nonsense operations specialist, stepped forward, his voice steady but laced with frustration.

"Sir, we have deployed five special teams working round the clock. But Aaron isn't surviving on his own, someone is helping him. We need to investigate Melvin, the CEO of Care All Technology. Without inside support, Aaron wouldn't have lasted this long."

Mylvaganan narrowed his eyes.

"Melvin is a powerful businessman. Unless we have rock-solid evidence, we can't touch him. And with the media breathing down our necks, we have to be careful. I hope you understand that."

Sreejith clenched his jaw, biting back his anger. "Understood, Sir."

"You have three more days." Mylvaganan's tone was final. "If you fail, the case goes to the CBI."

Just then, Sreejith's phone buzzed violently in his pocket. Irritated, Mylvaganan gestured for him to answer.

"Hello, Sreejith speaking!"

The voice on the other end rattled off something urgent. Sreejith's expression shifted from frustration to shock.

"What?! Stabbed to death?! Seal the crime scene, don't let a single word leak to the media. I'm on my way!"

Mylvaganan raised an eyebrow. "Now what?"

Sreejith exhaled sharply. "Sir... Shylesh, the administrator of Care All Technology, was found murdered in an abandoned building near Anna Flyover."

The room fell into a heavy silence.

Mylvaganan's expression darkened. "This is escalating fast. Go. Start the investigation. And remember, I want Aaron in as soon as possible."

As Sreejith rushed out, Mylvaganan straightened his uniform and strode toward the press waiting outside. He stepped in front of the microphones, his face unreadable.

"We have sealed all city exits. Every vehicle leaving Chennai is being checked. Five special teams under SP Sreejith are working tirelessly to capture the fugitive. The police force is fully committed to bringing him back behind bars."

The questions fired instantly.

"Why did Aaron go to the office?"

"Will Melvin be investigated?"

"With so many officers searching, how is he still managing to evade capture?"

Mylvaganan didn't flinch. Instead, he turned without a word, got into his car, and slammed the door shut.

Meanwhile, Sreejith slipped through the back exit, heading straight to the crime scene.

Abandoned Building, Chennai…

Murder scenes always have a certain… predictability. In movies, they happen in dimly lit, desolate buildings. In reality? Those places exist. They're hotspots for illegal deals, drug exchanges, and sometimes, they're just a shelter for the homeless. But tonight? Tonight, this building was a slaughterhouse.

The air was thick with the metallic stench of blood. The dull flickering of a single streetlight outside cast eerie shadows across the crime scene.

Sreejith stepped in, accompanied by **Inspector Anwar**. His voice was sharp.

"Brief me."

Anwar glanced at his notes. "Victim sustained five stab wounds, two in the cervical region, three in the abdomen. Additionally, we found hand marks around his neck."

Sreejith's eyes narrowed. "Strangled and stabbed? Someone held him from behind while another person attacked. There were two killers."

"Yes, Sir. Based on blood patterns, the victim tried to escape after being dragged here. The cervical stabs suggest he was attacked while running. No shoe prints, no murder weapon recovered."

Sreejith looked around. "Tire marks outside?"

Anwar sighed. "No, Sir. Heavy rain this morning washed away any traces."

"CCTV footage from the nearest signal?"

"Nothing useful. No suspicious movement detected."

Sreejith ran a hand over his face. This case is spiralling out of control.

"Finalize the report and bring the autopsy details to my house this evening."

He turned to leave, then suddenly stopped.

"Did we recover his phone?"

Anwar hesitated. "No, Sir. There was no phone found on him."

Sreejith's gaze sharpened. "He didn't have it? Or the killer took it?"

Anwar stiffened.

"Pass this to the cyber department. Monitor his number. If that phone comes online, I want to know immediately."

"I'll handle it right away, Sir."

Sreejith exhaled, stepping outside into the cool night air. He had a bad feeling about this. This wasn't just another murder. This was a message.

And someone was making damn sure they stayed ten steps ahead.

Chapter 14

Safe House…

The birds outside chirped endlessly, oblivious to the storm inside me. I sat there, frozen in the centre of the dimly lit safe house. I hadn't eaten. I hadn't refreshed. I hadn't even moved.

Memories of Gilbert flashed in my mind like a cruel, relentless slideshow. His laughter, his words, his loyalty or what I thought was loyalty. It was gut-wrenching to realize that all this time, he had been acting.

People talk about heartbreak in love, but friendship? Friendship cuts just as deep. Care. Trust. Affection. Respect. Forgiveness. Possessiveness. Humour. Open communication. Every element of love is there… except for intimacy.

And betrayal? It's the sharpest knife of them all. I took a deep breath, gripping the pocketknife in my hand. A loud knock shattered my thoughts. Instinct kicked in.

I moved silently to the peephole, my muscles tense. It was Jennifer.

I had left her a letter, a hidden message with instructions on where to find me. Slowly, I unlocked the door, letting her in. The moment she stepped inside, she crushed me in an embrace, holding me so tight I could feel my ribcage strain.

But none of that mattered.

I buried my face in her shoulder, the scent of her hair filling my senses. For the first time in days, I let my walls collapse, my tears soaking into her skin. We sat down, and I told her everything.

She listened, calm, steady, but her eyes burned with the same fire that had ignited in mine.

"I understand how you're feeling," she said, voice raw with emotion. "My father was an honest man. Respected by everyone. He ran a business with his best friend, someone he trusted with his life. But one day, that 'friend' forged documents, took a 10-crore loan in the company's name, and vanished. We lost everything. My father... he couldn't bear it. He died drowning in the weight of that betrayal."

She swallowed hard, steadying herself. "Our uncle took us in, but at a price. He forced my mother to marry him. She did it for me, to raise me. And now, Aaron...

you have a responsibility too. As a son. As a husband. You need to clear your name."

She looked straight into my soul.

Determination surged through me. "I will."

Jennifer exhaled, finally allowing herself to smile. "Good. Now go freshen up. I brought food. You need to eat."

For the first time in what felt like forever, my lips curled into a genuine smile.

"What would I do without you?"

She turned away quickly, pretending to check her bag, but I caught it, the faintest, most beautiful smile spreading across her face. That smile... it could shatter a man, rebuild him, and then destroy him all over again.

I took a long, cold shower, washing away the fatigue, the anger, the pain. When I stepped out, a towel wrapped around my waist, Jennifer's eyes flickered toward me before quickly looking away.

"Come on, eat," she said, her voice a little softer than before.

I moved behind her, my presence lingering close. She froze. Her breathing hitched, her hands tightening around the plate.

She felt me before she saw me.

I wrapped my arms around her waist, pulling her into me. She didn't resist.

I leaned in, pressing a slow, lingering kiss an inch below her neck. She gasped, her body shivering under my touch, before turning towards me.

And then we lost ourselves.

Our lips met in a feverish hunger, a collision of longing, frustration, and relief. Her fingers traced slow, teasing patterns along my back, pulling me deeper into her. My hands roamed, pulling her closer until there was no space left between us.

The world ceased to exist.

There was no chase. No betrayal. No danger.

Just us.

We dressed, the air between us thick with unspoken words. We had just sat down to eat when a knock at the door cut through the silence.

Jennifer stiffened, fear flashing in her eyes.

I rose, knife gripped in my hand, and moved toward the door. My heartbeat thundered, preparing for the worst.

But as I opened it, I froze.

It was my parents, Hamshad, and Mandeep.

"How did you...?" I started, but Hamshad was already answering.

"Jennifer left a note on my desk before sneaking out of the office. I knew she was up to something. And your parents? They haven't stopped crying since this started. I had to bring them."

I turned to see my mother's tear-streaked face, my father's worried gaze. A lump formed in my throat.

"Mom, Dad… it's not safe here. You need to leave…"

Before I could finish, Mandeep, usually the clown, stepped forward with a rare seriousness.

"We're not going anywhere. We're staying. We'll fight this with you."

I clenched my jaw, shaking my head. "You don't understand. They're planning ahead, moving faster than I can. Every step I take, they're already waiting."

A deep voice cut through the tension.

"That's because there was a mole before. But now?" My father, a seasoned military man stepped forward. His presence shifted everything. "Now, we plan. And we execute."

Jennifer grinned, flashing all 32 of her perfect teeth. "Mom and Dad deserved to know what's happening. They needed to see you."

I shook my head, exhaling sharply.

For the first time in days, the weight didn't feel so suffocating. The energy in the room shifted, I wasn't alone anymore.

I wasn't going to lose.

"No more arguing," I said, looking at Hamshad and Mandeep. "I have a plan."

As I spoke, one thought burned in my mind. When a friend or a lover betrays you, it's not the end.

It's the beginning.

The moment life teaches you to separate actors from amigos.

And if you have a true friend, a friend who doesn't need to be called by name, who listens without judgment, who brings you out of darkness, who fights by your side even when you're wrong, then you have everything.

I clenched my fists, eyes burning with renewed purpose.

"It's time to start our hunt... and bring them down."

Chapter 15

The Hunt Begins…

Gilbert is the first target.

The plan was simple: trap the rat inside the cage.

Unlike most people, Gilbert still used an old-school, non-smartphone model—something that worked to our advantage. He had no access to internet banking, no instant balance checks, and worst of all, no clue about tech tricks.

And we were about to exploit that.

Mandeep once used an SMS API software to trick Seby into thinking she lost Rs. 20,000 from her account when we were at the theatre. Gilbert wasn't with us that day, meaning he had no idea about the trick. That ignorance would be his downfall.

Once we sent the fake SMS about a withdrawal from his account, he would panic. He wouldn't call customer service as he was terrible at handling things like that. Instead, he'd rush to the nearest ATM to check his balance.

There were two ATM locations near his house, both rarely occupied.

Mandeep would stake out one with a Midazolam injection, a powerful sedative. Hamshad and I would cover the second ATM with the same weapon. Thanks to Jennifer's friend, we managed to get our hands on Midazolam, something that wasn't easy to acquire.

Everything was in place.

We split into two teams and took our positions near the ATMs, staying in touch through new burner phones and Bluetooth earbuds.

The trap was set.

The SMS was sent. Now, we just had to wait for the rat to sniff its way into danger.

"Be alert, Mandeep," I whispered through the mic.

"Alert? Bro, I swear I'm about to pee myself."

"Come on, Mandeep. We're positioned here because there's a higher chance of him showing up at this ATM. Just breathe and stay calm."

"Aaron, I assume you failed probability in college?"

"What?"

"Because he's walking towards my ATM."

I stiffened. "Take him down. We're five minutes away… we'll be there to help."

"Copy that."

I could hear Mandeep's heavy breathing through the earpiece. I knew he was nervous, but we had no time for doubts. This had to go smoothly. Gilbert approached the ATM cautiously. Mandeep moved in. He sneaked behind him, gripping the syringe. And then, something went wrong.

Gilbert stopped abruptly.

He turned around, scanning the area. Mandeep barely had time to duck behind a parked Bolero, pressing his bulky frame against the metal. After a few seconds, Gilbert seemed to relax and entered the ATM booth. Mandeep inhaled deeply. This was it. The moment to strike. He started moving toward the booth, fingers tightening around the syringe.

But just as he was about to step in. Gilbert walked right out. He didn't even take out his card. Instead, he turned and started walking in the opposite direction. Mandeep frowned, confused. He hesitated, then crept toward the ATM. And that's when he saw it.

"OUT OF SERVICE."

"Guys, emergency… he's coming toward your ATM!"

Hamshad's irritated voice crackled through the earpiece. "What are you blabbering, Mandeep?"

"The ATM here is out of service! He's heading your way!"

Hamshad swore. "Shit! Mandeep, take the car and meet us… NOW."

We had no choice but to adjust on the fly. Hamshad and I took deep breaths, pressing ourselves against the tree line. Our palms were sweaty, our pulses racing. We weren't professional kidnappers. We weren't trained for this. But we were about to cross a line that couldn't be undone.

Gilbert approached, his expression still clouded with suspicion. I stepped forward, blocking his path.

He stopped dead in his tracks, his face twisting in shock. "Aaron? What the hell are you doing here? Haven't you done enough?"

I clenched my jaw. "Not even close."

I lunged forward, syringe in hand. Gilbert's instincts kicked in, he grabbed my wrist before I could drive the needle into his skin. We struggled, my grip tightening, his strength pushing back. He was strong, but not strong enough.

From behind, Hamshad struck. The needle pierced Gilbert's neck. His eyes widened in shock, mouth opening to scream, but nothing came out.

Within seconds, his body went limp. Mandeep pulled up just in time, tires screeching. We hauled Gilbert's deadweight into the back seat and slammed the door shut. We had him.

As the car sped toward the safe house, my heart was pounding. That was our first real mission. It was messy. It was terrifying. And it was successful.

I stared out the window, still catching my breath. How do professional criminals pull this off flawlessly? I exhaled sharply. No matter. We had Gilbert now.

And this was just the beginning.

The hunt was officially on.

Chapter 16

"This is a strong sedative. He hasn't even twitched," Mandeep muttered, nudging Gilbert's limp body with his foot.

"He's in for a surprise," Hamshad replied, smirking.

I was done waiting. I grabbed a bucket, filled it to the brim, and dumped the ice-cold water onto Gilbert's face. He jolted awake, gasping for air. His eyelids fluttered, struggling against the weight of the drug still coursing through his system. His vision was hazy, his consciousness flickering between reality and the fog of sedation.

I tapped his cheeks lightly at first, then harder to snap him out of it. Slowly, recognition dawned in his weary eyes as he took in the sight before him.

Mandeep grinned. "Welcome, Mr. Gilbert."

Gilbert's gaze hardened. "You idiots have no idea what you're doing. If Melvin finds out, he'll wipe you all out."

I crouched down, locking eyes with him. "He's not coming for you. Don't worry."

Gilbert scoffed. "You don't understand. He needs me. We're closer than you think."

"Are you sure about that?" I gestured toward Hamshad, who pulled out his phone and played an audio recording.

Melvin's voice crackled through the speaker.

"Who is this?"

"Aaron here. I have a surprise for you."

Melvin chuckled. "You're the only one who's survived this long in my 25-year career. Okay, tell me... what's the surprise?"

A notification sound. The recording continued.

"Is this the best you've got? Trapping your ex-friend to threaten me? Did you really think this would work?"

Silence.

Then Melvin's voice, colder now.

"After this is over, I planned to kill him myself. But since you've saved me the trouble, go ahead. Finish him off. I'll send the payment."

My blood boiled. "Melvin!" I had screamed in the recording.

"Shut up and hang up the phone. Enjoy the little time you have left."

The recording ended. I watched as Gilbert's face shifted from defiance to disbelief. The betrayal had sunk in.

"Is this the man you thought would save you?" I asked.

He lowered his head. For the first time, he had nothing to say. I signalled to Hamshad to start video recording.

"Tell me everything, Gilbert. Keeping your mouth shut won't save you. Melvin will kill you either way. But if you talk, we might be able to make a plan."

His misty eyes met mine. "Where do I even begin?"

"Start from the beginning. That's the only way we end this."

Gilbert exhaled shakily. "When Gopal Varma died, I knew something wasn't right. I sat beside him for months, he confided things in me. One day, he told me he had received an email by mistake. It was from Melvin... an insight into his black-market business."

"Black market?"

Gilbert nodded. "Before he could do anything, his entire system was wiped clean. When he confronted Melvin, he was given an offer. He refused. And that's why he died."

I clenched my fists. "So it was never a suicide."

"No. And I made the mistake of sharing this with Shylesh. One day, Shylesh sent me a message... Melvin wanted to see me. I was terrified. But when I walked into his office, everything changed."

"Changed how?"

"He offered me a deal... Rs. 20 lakh."

Mandeep's voice was sharp. "Let me guess. You took it. You didn't care about Gopal's family. His wife. His kids."

Gilbert swallowed hard. "I needed the money. And at the time, it felt like a way out."

"It wasn't," I said coldly.

"No, it wasn't. It was just the beginning."

He hesitated before continuing. "Melvin called me to his beach house one day. He explained how we would trap you, Aaron. I resisted at first. But when he doubled the amount, I agreed."

Mandeep scoffed. "So you'd do anything for money?"

"Even if I didn't, someone else would have," Gilbert said bitterly. "At least this way, I was in control."

I shook my head. "You're just justifying your betrayal."

His lips pressed together. Then, after a moment, he continued.

"But that's not all Melvin is involved in."

My father, who had been silently listening, stiffened. "What do you mean?"

Gilbert's voice dropped. "He doesn't just run a black-market business. He steals patient information. Sells it. And in some cases, he's involved in human trafficking. Organ trade."

A chill ran down my spine.

"But that's not even the worst part," Gilbert continued. "Melvin has spies inside military bases. They feed him classified intelligence."

My father's face paled. "Aaron... we thought the military was protecting us. If this is true, even the military isn't safe anymore."

"Exactly," Gilbert whispered. "And I overheard something even worse. I don't know who he's working with, but whatever they're planning... it's bigger than anything we've imagined."

"We need proof," I said. "We have to take Melvin down."

Gilbert exhaled. "That's not easy. He has people from the bottom tier to the top, loyalists who would die for him. He has no known weaknesses."

"There has to be a way."

Gilbert hesitated. Then: "His laptop. Not the company-issued one. His personal one."

"Where is it?"

"At his beach house. Usually kept in a hallway locker. But the PIN is unknown."

Mandeep leaned forward. "We don't need the whole laptop. Just the SSD or HDD. If the laptop disappears, he'll know something's up."

I nodded. "Then that's our next move. We pull the rabbit out of the hole."

Gilbert looked at me, desperation in his eyes. "Please, Aaron. Help me. I'm sorry for everything."

I studied him. "Do you really think trust is that easy?"

He flinched.

I leaned in. "You should also know, the recording we played was fake. Made through a voice modulator. Melvin doesn't even know you're missing."

Gilbert's expression turned to rage. "I'll kill every one of you!"

I smirked. "It's too late. We've recorded everything. You have two choices: spend your life in prison and change for the better... or we send this video to Melvin and let him deal with you."

Gilbert trembled. "Aaron... think about my family."

My voice was steel. "Did you think about Gopal Varma's family? My family? Our friendship?"

Silence.

"You have to face the consequences, Gilbert. There's no other way."

As I looked at him, I didn't see an enemy. I saw a broken man who had lost himself chasing shortcuts to success. This wasn't just about revenge. It was about justice.

Gilbert exhaled shakily. "I will never forgive you for this."

I met his gaze. "One day, you'll understand. I still believe there's a good part of you left in there."

Because if there wasn't… Then he is already dead.

Chapter 17

Devising a plan to trap a rat is easy, but what about when we are the ones caught in a web spun by evil? And more importantly, how do you trap the devil himself? There was only one shot at this. Zero margin for error.

"We don't have that much time," Hamshad warned, his voice edged with urgency.

Mandeep smirked. "Thinking like a cop was easy for the first plan. But this? This is theft. Now, he needs to think like a thief."

His words, though spoken in jest, sparked something… a new plan taking shape in my mind.

Without wasting a second, I accessed my iCloud to retrieve a contact. Reva, the guy I met at the theatre. He owed me one. I dialled his number without hesitation.

"Hello, Reva?"

"Yes. Who is this?"

"Aaron. We met at the theatre during that incident. You gave me your number, said to call if I ever needed help."

A brief pause. Then, "I don't know anyone named Aar... wait! Yeah, I remember now. What do you need?"

"We need to take something from someone's house. And we need to do it now."

"Give me the details."

I relayed the location and specifics. The thing about thieves? Their minds work fast when an offer is placed on the table. And the thing about friendships? The gold chains we wear are always up for sale in times of emergency. Without hesitation, I took off Mandeep's ornament and set the price, 32 grams of gold.

The deal was struck. After the job, Reva would drop the item at a secure location.

"This plan better work," I muttered, fingers crossed.

The Heist Begins...

A delivery van sped toward Melvin's beach house. The sudden arrival caused an immediate stir. We observed from a safe distance, hidden behind thick vegetation. Planting trees? Not just for the environment, they also make excellent cover.

Two guards stood at the entrance. That alone spoke volumes about the wealth inside.

"Hey! You can't stop here. Get moving!" one of the guards barked.

Reva's men, calm as ever, replied, "There's a delivery for Melvin."

"We weren't informed about any delivery. Come back in three hours when our boss is available."

"Sir, we've come a long way. We can't take it back. Call your boss. We'll just place the fridge inside and leave."

Meanwhile, Mandeep, armed with a voice modulator, had flooded Melvin's personal number with calls from a fake agency. A lottery prize—a high-end refrigerator. At first, Melvin resisted. But relentless calls chipped away at his patience. Eventually, he instructed his guards to verify the agency.

The guards, unknowingly walking into our trap, confirmed the information at Hamshad's uncle's shop. With no choice left, Melvin reluctantly agreed to accept the fridge, just to stop the incessant calls.

The delivery was permitted. The fridge was placed inside. And hidden within it, was Reva.

Connected via Bluetooth, Reva whispered, "I'm inside. Leaving the fridge now."

He slipped out from the vegetable storage compartment and scanned the room. Then he froze.

"The laptop, it's right here. Just sitting on the table."

My gut clenched. "Describe it."

"Looks like an old Dell. Worn out."

I exhaled. "That's the office laptop. We need the one in the safety locker."

"Found it."

The real prize, the laptop that held the key to Melvin's operations is locked away.

Reva chuckled. "After all that hype, I thought this was going to be tough. The emergency key is right behind the locker."

I stiffened. "No! Don't use it."

"What? Why?"

"It's a trap. If you use the emergency key, an alarm will trigger. I read about a similar setup online. Use the other method."

Reva set the key aside and got to work. A fine layer of nano-powder spread over the dial, revealing faint fingerprints. Carefully, he analysed the intensity of the impressions, deducing the number combination.

Sweat dripped down his face.

"I think I've got it. Trying it now."

Four soft clicks echoed through the phone. Then silence.

"Reva?"

A beat passed. Then, "Got it. Removing the SSD. I'll be back in the vegetable box in twenty minutes. Send the van for extraction."

"On it."

The van returned. "Sir, we're swapping the fridge. It's a double-door model worth ₹80,000. Just a small mix-up."

Irritated but uninterested, the guards let them in. The switch happened in seconds.

Mission accomplished.

The Double Crosser...

Reva's location was set. We arrived, expecting an easy exchange. Instead, we found ourselves surrounded by thugs.

He smirked, holding up the SSD. "Here's the gold chain."

Reva scoffed. "You think I'm stupid? This SSD is worth way more than that. I want more."

My jaw tightened. "We trusted you. Don't do this."

He leaned in. "If I return this to Melvin, I'd get a fortune."

A slow laugh escaped my lips. "A fortune?"

His face darkened. "You find that funny? I can have you all killed in seconds."

I stepped closer, lowering my voice. "You think Melvin will make a deal with you? Sure, he'll take the SSD. But once he has it, he'll erase you and your entire crew. You know how he works."

Reva hesitated. His bravado wavered.

"Give us the SSD," I continued. "I'll make sure you're rewarded. Trust me."

His jaw clenched, but his hands loosened. With one last scowl, he tossed the SSD over.

Greed. Selfishness. Two traits that shape a person's destiny, either lifting them up, dragging them down, or turning them into monsters like Melvin. We secured the SSD and got into the cab, heading toward our safe house.

Then, Mandeep's phone rang.

We all froze.

Something wasn't right.

Chapter 18

Mandeep's hands trembled violently as he stared at the screen, Melvin's name flashing like a death sentence. A cold wave of dread crashed over us. Melvin had Mandeep's number. That wasn't supposed to be possible. Only those closest to him knew it. The walls were closing in. Our instincts screamed: **this was a trap.**

I slammed my palm against Mandeep's back, snapping him out of his trance. With his breath shallow and erratic, he hesitantly pressed 'accept' and lifted the phone to his ear.

"Hel... Hell... Hello," he stammered, voice barely above a whisper.

"Give the phone to him."

A slow exhale escaped my lips as I took the phone from Mandeep's cold, sweaty grip. Hesitation gripped my throat, but I forced myself to press the phone against my ear. "I'm listening."

A deep, amused chuckle slithered through the speaker. "Wow. Fantastic. You know, I love surprises. Do you want to take a wild guess where I am right now? Guess correctly, and maybe I won't paint the walls with your family's blood."

A steel grip clenched around my lungs. "Please... leave them alone."

Melvin clicked his tongue in mock disappointment. "Ah-ah, wrong answer. I hate when people don't play my games properly. Try again."

I squeezed my eyes shut, praying I was wrong. "... You're at our hideout."

A delighted laugh erupted on the other end. "Bingo! You're smarter than I thought. And since I'm feeling generous, I'll even tell you how I got here. See, I came home early today. Lucky, right? The thing about me is, I notice things. Even the tiniest details. The emergency key to my locker is always behind the safe, not beside it. And when I turned on my laptop? It screamed at me, 'missing drive.' Now, I'm not a paranoid man, but when I called Gilbert and his phone was conveniently dead, I decided to check the tracker on his leg. Guess where it led me? Straight to your cozy little hideout. And, oh, what a lovely reunion it's been! Your dad, your mom, Jennifer... and of course, our dear friend Gilbert."

My knees nearly gave out. "Leave them alone. Don't hurt them."

A long, contemplative pause. Then, in a voice as cold as death itself, he said, "See, I wanted to, but the demon inside me insists that I start with Gilbert first."

"Melvin, **NO—**"

BANG!

A gunshot tore through the night, followed by blood-curdling screams. My entire body went numb. My ears rang.

"Melvin! Don't do this! I swear, if there's even a scratch…"

A low chuckle slithered through the line. "Scratch? No, no, no. Gilbert's dead. That traitor doesn't get to breathe my air. I have a simple rule—'Loyal people don't deserve to live.' Cry about it later. Right now, I need my beauty sleep. Meet me at Karikattu Kuppam at 6 AM sharp. Don't worry… there aren't any ghosts there."

The line went dead.

Mandeep's voice was a blur, drowned out by the deafening static in my head. Gilbert was dead. My family was in his grasp. Before I could spiral any further, a brutal slap across my face snapped me back to reality.

"Focus, Aaron!" Hamshad roared. "We give him the information. We get them back. That's it! Understand?"

I took a shaky breath. "Mandeep, can we transfer the data to another drive?"

Hamshad's fury boiled over. "Are you serious right now?! Your family is going to die, and you're worried about some files? What the hell is wrong with you?!"

I turned to him, my gaze like steel. "What's wrong with me? Do you know how many people are trafficked for their organs because of that data? How many soldiers are fighting for us, not knowing there's a traitor among them? This isn't just about my family. If we throw away this information, we're no better than Gilbert."

Silence. Then, in a small, broken voice, Hamshad whispered, "I'm sorry, Aary. I let my emotions take over."

Mandeep's hands flew over his laptop. "Bad news. The drive is encrypted. Minimum ten hours to crack it."

"We don't have that much time. We'll figure something out on the way."

Karikattu Kuppam - 6:00 AM...

The air was thick with the stench of salt and dread. The moment an Audi SUV pulled up, an unsettling stillness took over the area. And then, he stepped out.

Melvin.

Dressed in crisp black, exuding an aura of untouchable arrogance, he strutted forward like a king surveying his kingdom. His sharp gaze dissected us, savouring every ounce of our fear.

He smirked. "I could shoot you all right here and take the information. But no, that would be too easy. You've given me quite the headache, Aaron. No, I want you to rot in a U.S. prison where you'll wish I had just killed you."

I swallowed hard. "Let them go. I'll give you what you want."

With a lazy wave of his hand, Jennifer and my mom were released. They stumbled towards me, sobbing. At the same time, Hamshad took slow, measured steps toward Melvin, holding the package containing the drive.

Melvin's greedy fingers snatched it up. He tore it open and examined the drive, a wicked grin spreading across his face.

"I'll be leaving now," he said smoothly. "On my way out, I'll drop your father from the car."

Panic flooded me. "No!"

He slid back into the car. I ran after it, my legs burning with desperation.

Inside the car, my father, his hands bound. Like the soldier he once was, he fought. His fingers scraped against the drive packet beside the charging port, reaching for it.

CRACK!

Melvin's fist smashed into his face. A gunshot followed.

Then, the door swung open, and my father was shoved out like trash.

His body hit the pavement, rolling like a discarded rag doll. The car screeched away as a gathering crowd rushed toward him. Blood pooled beneath him.

Police sirens echoed in the distance. We had to go.

Jennifer and my mom pulled me back, their screams mixing with mine. My body fought, thrashed, but they wouldn't let me go. I wasn't ready to let him go. Through blinding tears, we escaped into the shadows, heading to Seby's house for cover.

The nightmare was far from over.

Chapter 19

We reached Seby's house, a place that should have felt safe, but the air was thick with exhaustion and despair. She was alone, her parents living abroad, and we had nowhere else to go. I walked straight into the bathroom, turned the tap on full blast, and screamed into the void of rushing water. The frustration, the helplessness, it all needed to escape my body somehow. No one knocked, no one spoke. They all knew why I was doing this.

When I stepped out, my face drenched in cold water, the living room was silent except for the flashing news on TV:

"Data thief's father shot in ECR, currently in ICU."

Jennifer, her voice heavy with defeat, spoke first.

"We can't fight anymore. We're out of options. Either we surrender or we die. Those are the only two choices left."

I shook my head, the weight of my own thoughts crashing down like an avalanche. "He'll come to us again. We wait."

Jennifer's eyes locked onto mine, suspicion creeping into her tired gaze. "What did you do, Aaron?" Her hands grabbed my face, forcing me to hold eye contact.

I exhaled slowly. "We switched the drive."

A beat of silence. Then confusion. Then shock.

"He had no time to check the contents, no way to verify beyond the serial number. We swapped the tag on Mandeep's SSD, giving us time to crack the real drive."

The room was still. No one spoke. Even the air felt heavier.

Let him come for the final dance.

Ring...

The phone rang. I let it ring twenty times before I picked up.

"Hello! Is it the devil himself?"

"Aaron," Melvin's voice was venomous. "You've tested my patience long enough. I'm going to finish every single one of you. That's a promise."

"Calm down. Let's make a deal."

"A deal?" A dry laugh echoed through the phone. "You should've led with that earlier. What do you want?"

"250 million dollars."

Silence. Then, incredulous laughter. "Do you even know how much money that is?"

"I do. And I also know the worth of the stolen patient records from Kenver Cancer Care Institute."

His laughter stopped. His tone darkened. "Fine. I'll bring the money."

"Come alone. No tricks. Meet me at Thekarai Dam at 6 PM. **No ghosts there, don't worry.**"

"…Nice one."

As I hung up, all eyes were on me.

"That money's not for us," I clarified before anyone could speak. "Mom and Jennifer stay here. Hamshad, Gundu, get ready. Tonight, we end this."

Thekarai Dam, 6:00 PM…

The evening air was still, the water eerily calm, like it was holding its breath for what was to come. Melvin stood on the other side, waiting.

"Did you miss me?" he taunted.

I smirked. "Not really. But I figured I'd give you one last chance to be human."

His lips curled into a wicked grin. "Do you have the drive?"

I pulled it out, waving it slightly. "As much as I want to give this to you, I have something else for you too."

A flick of his wrist, and six of his best bodyguards stepped forward, guns trained on me.

"I knew you'd try this," I muttered.

Melvin chuckled. "Smart. But not smart enough."

"Guys, take him down."

They lunged.

The first strike landed, but I was ready. A quick step back, and I swung my electrified mosquito bat, sending sharp volts through the nearest thug. Another came at me, I ducked, swept his legs out, and slammed the bat into his ribs. But it wasn't enough. They overpowered me, slamming me to the ground, pinning me down as Melvin approached.

"You put up a good fight," he admitted. "But it's over."

The sound of sirens cut through the air. Red and blue lights flashed as the police swarmed the area, guns raised. Melvin's eyes flickered with something close to amusement before they landed on Gundu, who stood beside Superintendent Sreejith, handing over the real drive and Gilbert's video evidence.

Melvin took a step back, chuckling softly. "Well played."

Then, before anyone could react, he pulled a gun from his coat and aimed it, not at me, not at the cops, but at his own temple.

"Don't!" Sreejith shouted, stepping forward. "If you surrender, I can help you."

Melvin smiled calmly, undisturbed. "No one can help me. This is not the Farewell... but the dawn of something New."

A single gunshot shattered the silence. His body collapsed, blood pooling beneath him, the life leaving his eyes as the officers rushed forward.

Forensics was called in. The area was secured. And then, Sreejith turned to me.

"Great work," he said. "But you're under arrest."

Hamshad stepped forward, desperate. "Sir, he's done so much. Please..."

Sreejith's face softened slightly. "The law is the law. He escaped custody. He needs to be presented in court."

I exhaled. "What about my father?"

"He's out of danger. He's in the government hospital, recovering. You'll be able to see him soon."

Jennifer let out a small sob of relief, covering her mouth. Hamshad and Gundu stepped aside as the officers led me away.

Everything I endured in the past few days won't just fade into memory. Pain doesn't dissolve with time, nor does the weight of what we've done.

True friends aren't just names in our contact list. They become a part of our very existence. And when we leave this world, they don't stay behind, they travel with us, in memory, in spirit.

We call this existence 'life.' But most of us don't truly live it. We're stuck in a loop, trading real experiences for empty distractions. A computer screen isn't a life partner, yet for many, it's become one. We mistake digital validation for love. We remember a celebrity's birthday but forget the pain in the eyes of those closest to us.

Success used to be about growth. Now, it's about stepping on others to climb higher.

These aren't signs of progress. They're warnings of a world losing its way.

Real life isn't about louder voices, more replies, or constant noise. It's found in silence, the kind that listens. In presence, the kind that truly feels. In understanding, the kind that doesn't demand, but embraces.

Maybe then, we will finally start to live.

Chapter 20

Madras High Court...

As I walked through the grand doors of the courtroom, every step felt heavier than the last. My eyes darted across the room, scanning familiar faces—faces that had endured the storm with me.

My father, bruised but standing tall, raised a reassuring thumbs-up. A silent message: *I'm fine, son.* My friends lowered their heads in unison, an unspoken acknowledgment of our battle. *We did it.* Jennifer's eyes locked onto mine, holding back a flood of emotions. *Love. Relief. A promise.*

And my mother... Her tears were a language of their own, speaking of endless nights of worry, of prayers whispered into the void.

The court clerk's voice sliced through the air.

"Final Verdict for Case Number 108/5486XX."

I stepped into the victim's stand, my pulse drumming against my ribs. The judge's gaze was sharp, unreadable.

"After thorough examination of all evidence, in consultation with the American Medical Association representatives Martin and Elise, it is irrefutably proven that Mr. Melvin, the former President and Managing Head of Care All Technology, was the orchestrator of the patient data leaks. His greed led to the illegal trade of sensitive medical records for profit, violating both American and Indian law. However, with his self-inflicted death, legal retribution against him ceases."

A pause. The air in the courtroom was thick with anticipation.

"As a result, Care All Technology is hereby permanently banned in both India and the United States. Effective immediately, all office premises shall be sealed, and the company is mandated to provide a three-month salary advance to all employees to aid their transition."

My breath hitched. The battle wasn't just against Melvin, it was against an entire corrupt system. And now, that system was crumbling.

But the judge wasn't finished. His next words made my stomach drop.

"As for Aaron… while his actions were commendable, the court cannot, in good conscience, allow a precedent where individuals take justice into their own hands without consequences. Thus, he is sentenced to a fine of ₹50,000 and six months of community service at the Government Mental Care Unit."

A heavy silence followed. Then, the judge's expression softened ever so slightly. He gave me the smallest of smiles before standing and exiting the courtroom.

The verdict had been delivered.

The moment I stepped down from the stand, a tidal wave crashed into me, my friends, my family, Jennifer. Arms wrapped around me, crushing me in an embrace that stole the very breath from my lungs. It wasn't just relief. It was victory.

Sreejith approached, his usual stern demeanour intact.

"There are a few formalities left. Anwar, escort him to the custodial chamber."

I nodded. The storm had passed, but the scars would remain.

And yet, for the first time in a long time, the road ahead didn't feel so dark.

The Unveiling

The Custodial Chamber

Anwar led me into the custodial chamber, shutting the door behind me with a heavy thud. The room was dimly lit, the air thick with an eerie stillness. As I moved toward the round table at the centre, another door creaked open. Two pairs of shoes stepped in, their footsteps steady, deliberate.

Then... laughter. Loud, familiar, and unmistakably relieved.

I wasn't alone.

Across from me stood Vignesh Aacharya, my lawyer, and Sreejith, the Superintendent of Police.

Confused? Don't be. Let me bring you up to speed.

The turning point of this entire storm? A sick leave request.

Gilbert's clash with his team leader set off a chain reaction none of us saw coming. That very morning,

I received an unexpected call from the SP's office. That was when I met Sreejith, the man who would change everything.

"We need someone inside Care All Technology," he had said. "We need to know where their money is really coming from. And we need answers about Gopal Varma's death."

It wasn't an invitation. It was an assignment.

The conditions were brutal:

- I would work undercover.

- My first and only point of contact would be Sreejith himself.

- If my cover was blown, the police would deny any involvement.

- My entire appointment would remain classified until the operation was complete.

His final words still echoed in my mind: "We've been tracking your police applications and rejections for three years. You are exactly the kind of man we were looking for."

Everything after that? Carefully orchestrated deception.

- Vignesh visiting me behind bars? A setup for my escape, courtesy of the SP.

- The safe house I used as a hideout? An abandoned property belonging to Sreejith.

- The bathroom breakdown at Seby's house? Just a cover-up so I could call Sreejith undetected inquiring about my father and passing the drive to him.

- Mandeep delivering the drive? A crucial step in ensuring the operation's success.

- The final meet-up with Melvin? I had never planned to walk away from that unprepared.

Now, back to reality.

The three of us took our seats around the table, tension lingering like an unspoken truth.

Sreejith was the first to break the silence.

"The decrypted drive contains extensive transaction records... and a password-protected file. We're still working on cracking it, but the money trail? It all leads back to one person."

He slid a thick file across the table. Pages upon pages of documents, and on top of them... A photograph.

My next assignment.

Law Ends Here

Lawyer's House, Midnight 01:35 AM...

The dim glow of the TV flickered against the darkened walls, casting eerie shadows that danced to the slow, haunting rhythm of an 80s jazz melody. The saxophone's melancholic tune seeped through the air, weaving into the suffocating tension that filled the room.

A glass of whisky rested on the tea table, untouched.

Vignesh Aacharya sat on the sofa... bound, gagged, helpless. Sweat beaded across his forehead as his frantic, muffled screams drowned beneath the thick tape sealing his lips. His chest heaved, his breath ragged, his pulse pounding like a war drum.

To his left, a man sat with calculated ease.

Dressed impeccably in black, gloves shielding his hands, he reached for an apple from the fruit bowl. With a deliberate slowness, he retrieved a pocketknife from his pant pocket. The blade gleamed under the dim light as he sliced into the apple, consuming each piece with an unsettling serenity.

Then, a ringing sound.

From his pocket, he retrieved a satellite phone, placing it on the table. He tapped the speaker button. On the other end, a calm, almost melodic voice began to hum a tune. The humming stopped abruptly, giving way to an explosion of maniacal laughter.

Then came the voice, dripping with amusement and menace.

"Sorry, Aacharya, that I can't visit you in person. Do you know how tragic it is? Every soul who dares to cross my path is doomed to perish! No witnesses. No survivors. Only the echoes of their final breath remain."

Vignesh writhed against his restraints, his muffled screams turning to desperate, guttural noises. His eyes, wide with terror, pleaded for mercy—but mercy was never on the table.

The voice on the phone chuckled one last time.

"GO TO HELL!!"

Click. The line went dead.

And in the silence that followed…

The blade slashed across Vignesh's throat.

A spray of crimson. A gurgled choke. A final tremor of life.

His body slumped forward, motionless. The blood pooled beneath him, dark and endless, staining the floor like a cursed omen.

The man in black stood, adjusting his gloves. Without a second glance, he turned and disappeared into the night, leaving behind nothing but the remnants of a brutal, calculated execution.

To Be Continued…

The Central Thief
Raise of the Devil